P9-CCU-174

Pssst...
When baking a
birthday cake, it is
tremendously helpful
to know where
to find...

...the
Sun!

EAST

where the S

A Birthday Cake

Harcourt, Inc.

Orlando Austin New York San Diego Toronto London

Is No Ordinary Cake

Written and illustrated by

Debra Frasier

Requests for permission to make copies of
any part of the work should be mailed to the
following address: Permissions Department,
Harcourt, Inc., 6277 Sea Harbor Drive,
Orlando, Florida 32887-6777.

www.HarcourtBooks.com

Library of Congress Cataloging-in-Publication Data
Frasier, Debra.
A birthday cake is no ordinary cake/written and
illustrated by Debra Frasier.
p.   cm.
Summary: A lyrical recipe using the changes in the
natural world to explain to a child the time that
passes between one birthday and the next.
Includes recipe for more traditional birthday cake
as well.
[1. Year—Fiction. 2. Cake—Fiction.
3. Birthdays—Fiction.] I. Title.
PZ7.F8654Bir 2006
[E]—dc22   2005004194
ISBN-13: 978-0-15-205742-8
ISBN-10: 0-15-205742-0

First edition
H G F E D C B A

Printed in Singapore

The cut-paper collage illustrations in this book
were made with Canson paper.
The display and text type was set in Futura
DemiBold.
Color separations by Bright Arts Ltd., Hong Kong
Printed and bound by Tien Wah Press, Singapore
This book was printed on totally chlorine-free
Stora Enso Matte paper.
Production supervision by Pascha Gerlinger
Designed by Debra Frasier and Linda Lockowitz

With thanks to my editor, Allyn Johnston, superb Chef of Words;
to Julie Reimer, extraordinary cook, teacher, and cake tester;
to the always inventive bakers at Wuollet Bakery;
to the Steins, masters of the theme birthday;
and to the marvelous Calla,
who has shared eighteen birthday cakes with us

For all the Birthday Cake Bakers in the World

Bakers!

Tie your aprons!

Find your hats!

We have a birthday

cake to make!

A birthday cake is no ordinary cake.

Special ingredients are required.

Ladies and gentlemen,

meet

the Sun,

the first necessary ingredient

in any birthday cake.

No Sun. No cake.

The Earth spins

eastward

toward the Sun

to make morning,

then spins away,

making night.

One complete spin

equals

one complete day!

No spinning. No cake.

So hold on, bakers!

We're riding

the Earth

in a great

spinning circle

around the Sun,

from your birthday

to your

NEXT

birthday,

because

every circle

around the Sun

equals

ONE.

To start:

Collect the first sunrise

after your birthday.

If you're worried

you'll oversleep,

just point your bowl

eastward

the night before.

The morning Sun

will fill it right up.

You will need exactly 364 more sunrises, all clouds included.

Now, gather the following ingredients in the order they arrive.

Find the sound
of a returning red robin,
singing.
Simply open the window.
Your bowl will catch it.

Next—

stir in any two

bright spring

flowers.

Tulip.

Daffodil.

Azalea.

Crocus?

Mix well.

Add the sight of
a new bud turning green.
Grass. Leaf. Bush.
Look carefully.
Hold out your bowl.

At night,

look up often.

You will need to add at least

twelve full silver moons.

For extra sparkle,

catch one falling star

from any night sky.

Let ingredients sit.

Wait patiently.

Batter will thicken.

Find your bathing suit.

Ready? Pour in the slap of a wave hitting the sandy shore. Actually, the splash of any tumbling water will do.

Next— catch one hot summer wind from the south. Stir.

Add:

the shade

of two trees,

fully green,

found on

the longest day

of the year.

Let bowl sit.

Enjoy the wait.

Next—

wave two crisp red leaves
over your bowl. Discard.

Sprinkle in the

first cool fall morning

or, for snap,

a fire's crackle.

Now add the shadow
of a line of long-necked
geese, flying south.
A successful cake
can be made without one,
but you'll taste a
certain hard-to-describe
lightness if added.

Actually, any
south-flying bird's
shadow will do.

Experiment:
Try butterflies.

Again,

let batter sit.

Put on a sweater.

Stir often.

Find your mittens.

Next, catch the
the sound of
snowflakes
falling.
If there are
no snowflakes
in sight,
the sound of two shivers
substitutes nicely.

Keep your bowl warm
but not too hot.

Measure the shortest day you can find. (Check December 21st.) Add quickly.

Do not freeze.

And THEN,
after
collecting
your
365th
sunrise . . .

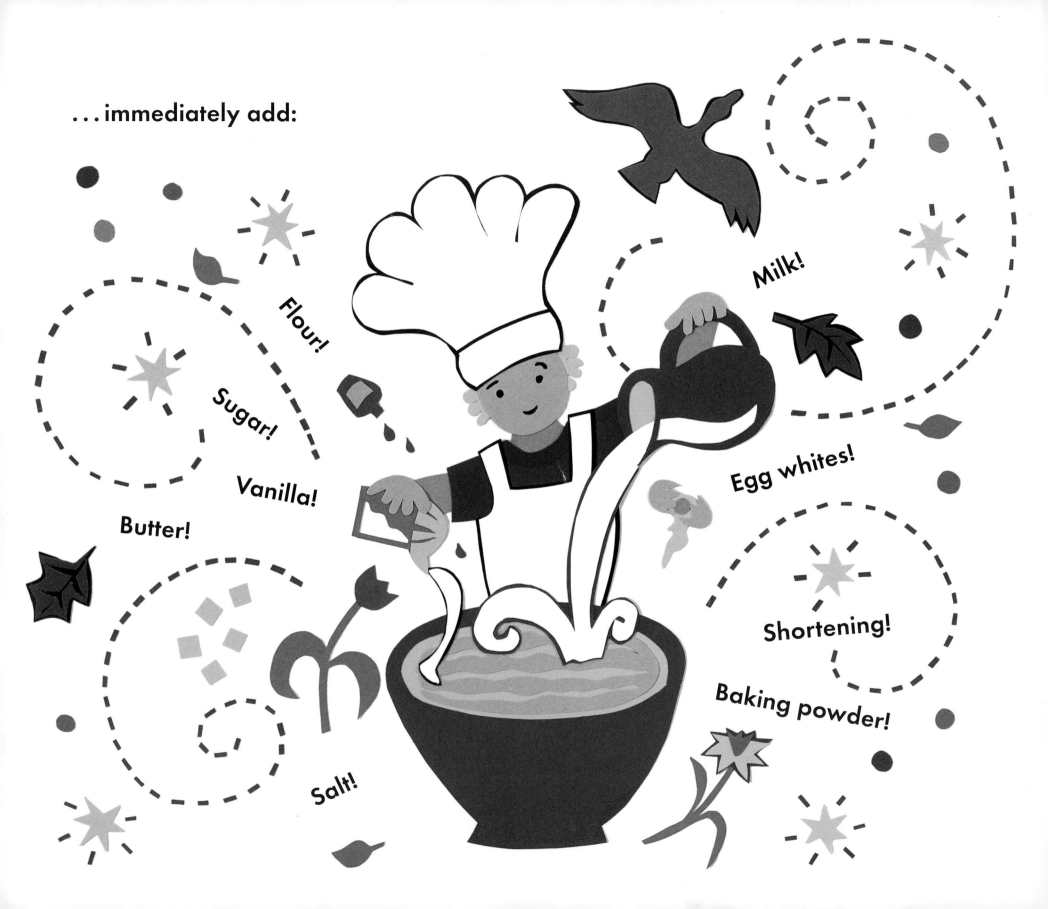

Stir. Sing.

Stir.

Pour in pans.

Bake.

Cool.

Ice.

Decorate with flowers.

Or snowflakes.

Or cowboys.

Or geese.

Lick the spoon.

At last, your cake is done!

Let's light a candle for

each time you've

circled

the

Sun.

We'll sing. You'll wish.

Then . . .

we'll cut the cake!

And remember—

we're traveling a circle.

This recipe is a circle.

It's all coming round again.

So before you

sleep . . .

. . . point
your bowl
eastward,

toward
the Sun.

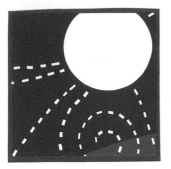

The Spinning World Birthday Cake

Preparation time: one year, exactly

Ingredients

365 sunrises
1 robin's song
1 greening bud
2 spring flowers
12 silver moons
1 falling star (optional)
1 wave (or tumbling water splash)
1 hot summer wind
Plenty of shade
2 crisp red leaves
1 cool fall morning
    (or substitute a fire's crackle)
Geese shadows, any amount
    (or substitute the shadow
    of any south-flying bird)
At least 1 snowflake's sound, falling
    (or the sound of two shivers)
1 shortest day

2$1/2$ cups all-purpose flour
1$3/4$ cups sugar
4 teaspoons baking powder
1 teaspoon salt
$1/2$ cup shortening
$1/2$ cup butter or margarine,
    at room temperature
2 teaspoons vanilla
1 cup milk
5 egg whites

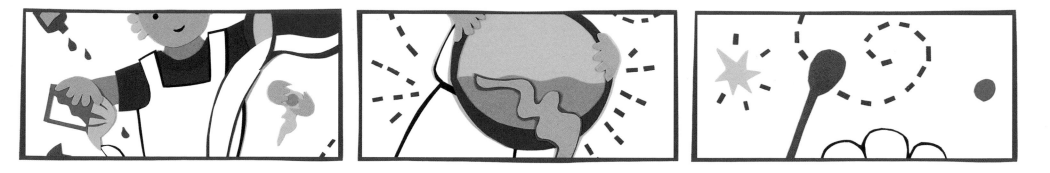

Preheat your oven to 350 degrees.

Grease and flour baking pan(s): 13 x 9 x 2 inch oblong or two round layer pans, 8-inch or 9-inch. Measure flour, sugar, baking powder, salt, shortening, butter, vanilla, and 2/3 cup of the milk into a large mixing bowl. Blend two minutes at slow speed, humming birthday songs, scraping bowl constantly. Then beat two minutes at high speed, scraping bowl occasionally. Add remaining milk and the egg whites. Again, beat two minutes at high speed, scraping bowl occasionally. Pour into prepared pan(s), spreading batter evenly.

Bake oblong cake 35–40 minutes, layers 30–35 minutes, or until top springs back when lightly touched in the center.

Cool. Sing again.

Creamy Vanilla Frosting

1/4 cup shortening	4 cups powdered sugar
1/3 cup butter, at room temperature	2 teaspoons vanilla
	2–4 tablespoons milk

Beat shortening and butter with an electric mixer at high speed for one minute or until well combined and fluffy. Add powdered sugar, vanilla, and two tablespoons of the milk. Beat at medium speed to combine, adding more milk until the frosting is creamy.

Spread on cooled cake(s) using a spatula.

Creamy Chocolate Frosting

1/2 cup butter, at room temperature	3/4 cup cocoa
3 1/2 cups powdered sugar	1 teaspoon vanilla
	4–6 tablespoons milk

Beat butter with an electric mixer at medium-high speed until fluffy. Add powdered sugar, cocoa, vanilla, and four tablespoons of the milk. Beat at low speed to combine, adding enough milk to make the frosting of spreading consistency. Beat at medium-high speed for one minute or until smooth.

Spread on cooled cake(s) using a spatula.

Counting Circles

The Sun

Even though we can't feel it, the Earth is constantly moving. It is rotating eastward, spinning in place like a top. We count each spinning rotation as a twenty-four-hour day. The Earth is also slowly orbiting around the Sun. It takes 365 days—or one year—for the Earth to complete this immense circle. We count these years by adding candles to our birthday cakes!

We are not the only species on the planet to be marking the days and years. Trees offer one of the most visible accountings. The living cell layer of a tree lies just under its bark. In the spring, these cells start responding to the increase in light and moisture of the warmer months and begin to grow. More sun and more rain encourage the growth of a wider band of cells. In the winter months, the cells die back, and then, each spring a new ring begins again.

A cedar tree

A *dendrochronologist,* a scientist who has learned to read the language of tree rings, finds a detailed weather journal in the cross section of a tree's trunk. (The rings of petrified log slices can reveal seasonal information from hundreds of millions of years ago.) Counting the rings of a tree's cross section is like counting birthday candles on a cake—one ring for each year. Similarly, underwater tropical corals add layers of calcium carbonate every day, making annual rings that can be counted and studied for information about water and light conditions in that part of an ocean.

What living thing has counted more circles around the Sun than any other? Bristlecone pines, some of which have quietly stood on the mountaintops of the western United States recording nearly 5,000 circles around the Sun.

Remember that no matter what, even while you are sleeping, the Earth keeps spinning and traveling around the Sun. Your birthday is always coming around again. Happy birthday to you! Happy birthday to everyone!

Key to the Map

— One day

— First day of each month

— The days of each month counted in fives (5th, 10th . . .)

— One for each year's two solstices (when the Sun is farthest from the equator) and two equinoxes (when the Sun crosses the equator, and day and night are approximately equal everywhere on Earth)

— Leap year day, February 29. This day is added once every four years because the Earth's rotation each day actually takes slightly more than twenty-four hours. After four years, enough "extra time" has been accumulated for one whole day, which is added to the calendar at the end of February.

Illustration notes: Neither the Earth nor the Sun nor the distances between them are pictured to scale in this book. The Sun's diameter is nearly 110 times greater than that of the Earth, and the Sun is 93 million miles (150 million kilometers) away.

Sun photo courtesy NASA/JPL-Caltec
Tree photo by Debra Frasier